Sophie Kinsella

Mummy Fairy and Me

Illustrations by Marta Kissi

PUFFIN

PUFFIN BOOKS

UK | USA | Canada | Ireland | Australia
India | New Zealand | South Africa

Puffin Books is part of the Penguin Random House group of companies
whose addresses can be found at global.penguinrandomhouse.com.

www.penguin.co.uk   www.puffin.co.uk   www.ladybird.co.uk

First published 2018
004

Text copyright © Sophie Kinsella, 2018
Illustrations copyright © Marta Kissi, 2018

The moral right of the author and illustrator has been asserted

Set in Bembo Infant MT Std
Text design by Mandy Norman
Printed in Great Britain by Clays Ltd, St Ives plc

A CIP catalogue record for this book is available from the British Library

ISBN: 978-0-141-37788-9

MIX
Paper from
responsible sources
FSC® C018179

Penguin Random House is committed to a
sustainable future for our business, our readers
and our planet. This book is made from Forest
Stewardship Council® certified paper.

For Rex and Sissy

CONTENTS

Meet Mummy Fairy and me

Hello. I'm called Ella Brook and I live in a town called Cherrywood. I have blue eyes and dark brown hair. My best friends at school are Tom and Lenka. My worst enemy is Zoe. She lives next door and she's my Not-Best Friend. She looks mean even when she smiles. You'll meet them all later.

And this is my mummy. She looks normal, like any other mummy . . . but she's not. Because she can turn into a fairy. All she has to do is stamp her feet three times, clap her hands, wiggle her bottom and say, 'Marshmallow' . . . and **POOF!** she's Mummy Fairy. Then if she says, 'Toffee apple,' she's just Mummy again.

I love it when she's Mummy Fairy because her wings shimmer like hundreds of rainbows. She wears a silver crown that shines like starlight. She can fly in the air and turn invisible and do real magic. Plus,

she's just bought a new wand that is really
cool. It's called the Computawand V5.
It has magic powers and a computer
screen *and* an Extra-Fast Magic button.

Most fairies have Computawands
nowadays. They have Fairy Apps and
Fairy Mail and even Fairy Games.
Mummy sometimes lets me look at the
apps and games if I've been good. (But she
always turns off the magic function first.)

★

My Aunty Jo and Granny look
normal, just like Mummy, but they

can turn into fairies too.

Aunty Jo has a Computawand V5 just like Mummy's. She can work the computer screen very fast and she knows every single spell code. Aunty Jo is very good at magic. She won Best Spell at the Fairy Awards.

Granny won't have a Computawand because she doesn't like anything that goes *bleep*. She still has an old-fashioned fairy wand with a star on top. She says it's never let her down yet, and she won Best Spell at the Fairy Awards with it three times in a row, and lots of other fairy prizes.

Mummy hasn't won any fairy prizes.

★

When she's not being a fairy, Mummy is a boss in an office. That means she tells people what to do. Mummy is very good at doing that. She's also very good at telling bedtime stories and singing songs in the car. She's the best mummy in the world.

But she's not very good at doing magic. You'll soon find out what I mean.

All the girls in my family turn into fairies when they're grown up, so one day

7

I will too. I'll have sparkly wings and my own Computawand. I can't *wait*. Mummy calls me her Fairy-in-Waiting.

I'm not allowed to start magic lessons yet, but I'm trying to learn anyway. Every week Mummy has magic lessons from Fenella, her Fairy Tutor, who talks to her on FairyTube. I watch with her and try my hardest to remember all the spell codes. Mummy tries very hard too. I'm sure she will get better one day.

When Mummy is not being a fairy, her Computawand just looks like a normal phone. Which is good because it is a big secret that Mummy is a fairy. No one must *ever* find out. I'm not allowed to tell anyone, not even my friends.

★

Ollie is my little brother. He's only one year old and he can't turn into a fairy. Everyone says he looks like me, but he doesn't because he's a

Weezi!

baby and I'm not a baby. He can't even speak properly. His favourite word is 'Weezi-weezi-weezi'.

*

And here's my daddy. He can't turn into a fairy either and he can't do magic. He says he can park the car instead.

FIXERIDOO!
The fixing spell mix-up and the Fairy Dust

It began on Saturday morning. We were having breakfast and Ollie grabbed the milk jug.

'Careful, Ollie!' said Mummy.

There is no point saying 'careful' to Ollie. He waved the jug around and it splashed on the table.

'Put it down!' I said. I tried to get the jug, but Ollie wouldn't give it to me.

'Give me the jug, darling,' Mummy said to Ollie. She tried to take it from him, but Ollie hugged it tighter, like a teddy. Mummy pulled his hands off, but Ollie grabbed it again . . . and suddenly the milk was all over the floor.

Ollie said, **'Weezi-weezi-weezi!'**

Mummy said, 'He doesn't know what he's doing.'

I think he *did* know what he was doing. The milk glugged all over the floor,

under the chairs and into the corners of the room.

'Never mind,' said Daddy. 'I'll pop to the supermarket.'

'That will take too long,' said Mummy.
'We need more milk right now.'

She stamped her feet three times,
clapped her hands, wiggled her bottom
and said, 'Marshmallow' . . . and
POOF! she was a fairy.

Every time Mummy turns into a fairy
I gaze at her. When Mummy is a fairy,
she is sparkly all over. She has beautiful
shimmery wings, and when they move
they send little breezes around. Even her
smile is more sparkly.

Mummy Fairy took her phone out of

her bag. As soon as she touched it, it started
to glow and grew into a Computawand.

'Are you sure about this?' said Daddy.

'Of course I'm sure!' said Mummy Fairy.
'You know I'm getting better at magic
every day.'

Daddy muttered something, but we
couldn't hear him properly.

'What?' said Mummy Fairy.

'Nothing,' said Daddy. 'Go ahead.'

Mummy Fairy pressed a code on the
screen – **bleep-bleep-bloop** – then waved
it and said, 'Milkeridoo!'

At once there was a cow in our kitchen. A great big brown cow with a bell round her neck.

'Oops,' said Mummy Fairy. 'I don't know how *that* happened.'

'Do you know how to milk a cow?' asked Daddy.

'No!' said Mummy Fairy. 'Of course I don't!'

'Moo!' said the cow.

The cow tried to walk round, but there wasn't room. So she flicked her tail and knocked all the apples out of the fruit

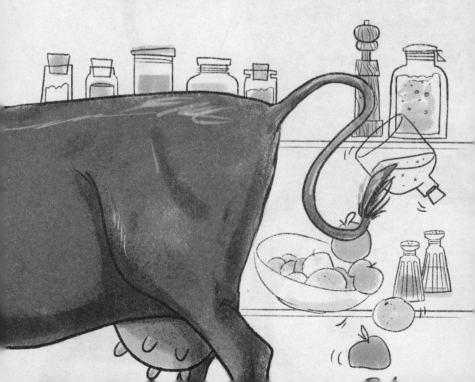

bowl. Then she broke three of Mummy's
favourite cups with the pink flowers.

'Stop that!' shouted Mummy Fairy, and

she steered the cow away. Then the cow pooed on the floor.

'For heaven's sake,' said Daddy.

'I'm sorry,' said Mummy Fairy. 'I'll try again.' She pressed a different code on her Computawand – *bleep-bleep-bloop* – and shouted, 'Milkeridoo!' for the second time.

The ceiling started to rain on us. It was brown rain and it went everywhere, all over our hair and our breakfast. I licked the rain off my chin and it was yummy.

'It's chocolate milk!' I said. 'It's raining chocolate milk! Yummy! Can we have this every day?'

'No, we can't,' said Mummy Fairy. She

looked up crossly at the brown rain. 'I
didn't want chocolate milk. And I didn't
want a cow. I just want a bottle of milk.
Stoperidoo!'

The rain stopped. Then Mummy Fairy pressed another code, shouted, **'Awayeridoo!'** and the cow disappeared too.

Daddy sighed. He squeezed some chocolate milk out of his hair. 'There's too much magic in this house,' he said.

'But it should have worked! I don't understand *what's* going wrong,' said Mummy Fairy. 'This Computawand is brand new. It has an Extra-Fast Magic button.' She pressed the button on her Computawand and it bleeped.

'Shall I try again?'

'**No!**' shouted Daddy. 'I mean . . .
why not go to the supermarket? We need
to buy some other food too.'

'But the supermarket is very slow,' said
Mummy Fairy. 'And I'm very busy today.
I've got lots of things I need to do.'

'More haste, less speed,' said Daddy.

'What does that mean?' I asked.

Daddy replied, 'It means, if you hurry
too much, things will go wrong. *Especially*
if you use magic.'

Daddy can't do magic or fly. He says,

'If you want to fly, why not get on a plane, like normal people?'

But Mummy isn't normal people. She's Mummy Fairy.

★

When we got to the supermarket, I saw Tom and Lenka.

'Hello, Lenka!' I called. 'Hello, Tom!'

Tom was pushing the trolley to the till for his mum. Tom is always doing kind things like that.

There was a lady doing face paints, and Lenka was having her face painted

like a butterfly, with silver glitter.

'Can I have my face painted like
Lenka?' I asked.

But Mummy shook her head. 'Sorry,
Ella, no time. Come on!'

We ran up the cereal aisle and Mummy grabbed boxes of cereal. We were going so fast that Ollie laughed and waved his hands, as if he was on a baby theme-park ride.

At the apple counter they were doing an apple-tasting. But Mummy said, 'Sorry, Ella, no time. Come on!'

We rushed around the supermarket with our trolley like runners in a race. Ollie sat in the front and Mummy sang, '*Ollie in the trolley, Ollie in the trolley.*'

But when we reached the checkouts Mummy stopped singing. She looked cross instead. There were *so many people*. They were all standing in lines, with full, full trolleys. One man was buying a hundred packets of soap powder!

Tom and his mum were leaving the shop with their bags of shopping. Tom saw us and he called, 'Good luck! We had to wait for *ages*.'

'Honestly!' said Mummy. 'Let's speed things along.'

I wasn't sure about that. I said, 'Do you remember what Daddy said? He said, "More haste, less speed."'

'Well, I have a lot to do today,' said Mummy. 'We need to hurry up . . .'

We went behind a rack of baked beans where no one else was. Very quietly Mummy stamped her feet three times, clapped her hands, wiggled her bottom and said, 'Marshmallow' . . . and **POOF!** she was a fairy.

Quickly she pressed a code on her Computawand – ***bleep–bleep–bloop*** – then pointed it at herself and said, **'Inviseridoo!'** Then no one could see her except me. I can always see Mummy when she's invisible because one day I will be a fairy too.

Mummy Fairy pressed another code on her Computawand screen – ***bleep–bleep–***

bloop – and pointed it at the lady at the till. **'Speederidoo!'** she shouted.

At once the lady loading her shopping started throwing things quickly into the trolley. 'There!' said Mummy Fairy. 'That's a lot better.'

A pineapple landed in the trolley – **thud!** A bag of crisps landed – *crinkle!* A barbecue landed – **crash!**

After a minute Mummy Fairy said, 'Let's speed things up even more.'

'Isn't this fast enough?' I said.

'The faster the better,' said Mummy Fairy.

She pointed her Computawand at all the ladies and men at the tills and pressed the Extra-Fast Magic button. **'Speederi-deederi-doo!'** she shouted.

All the ladies and men started throwing things quickly into their trolleys. They went faster and faster and faster.

'Mummy Fairy,' I said, 'I think this is *too* fast.'

Eggs flew through the air and landed – **smish-smash!** Bottles of lemonade thumped down and exploded

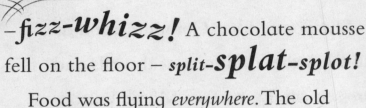

*–fizz-**whizz**!* A chocolate mousse fell on the floor – *split-**splat**-splot!* Food was flying *everywhere.* The old man in front of me got a stinky cheese on his head. One lady got broccoli stuck in her ear. Ollie was covered in baked beans and he laughed and laughed.

A tub of ice cream landed – *splat!* – and someone's dog ran in super fast and started licking it up off the floor until a shop lady chased it out.

Then the lady at the till started throwing the soap-powder packets into the trolley. **Boom!** *Boom! Boom!* They all burst open. Everything was covered in a big white powdery cloud. All the people looked like snowmen.

I wanted to laugh, but I felt worried too. Everyone was running around and screaming.

Mummy Fairy looked very alarmed. 'What do you think, Fairy-in-Waiting?' she said to me. 'What should I do?'

'Use the Fixeridoo spell,' I said.

I learned about the Fixeridoo spell from watching Mummy's magic lessons with Fenella on FairyTube. The Fixeridoo spell is the spell you use when things have gone really, really wrong. But it is so powerful that the Fairy Rule

Book says you can only use it once a
week.

'Do you remember how to use it?' I
asked Mummy Fairy.

'Of course I do!' said Mummy Fairy.
She pressed a code on her Computawand –
bleep–bleep–bloop – and waved it.

'Fixeridoo!' she shouted. But nothing
happened. 'Fixeridoo!' shouted Mummy
Fairy again. **'FIXERIDOO!'**

Food was still flying around in
the air. A pork pie hit me on the
head and I shouted, **'Ow!'**

'Ella, I can't fix it.' Mummy Fairy looked very worried. 'Help!'

'The Fixeridoo spell is easy-peasy!' I said.

I wondered if Mummy was using the right code. Mummy finds it hard to remember all the magic spell codes. She says her head is too full of other things, like raising a family and holding down a job.

'What numbers are you pressing on the Computawand?' I called.

'4–5–9,' said Mummy Fairy. She looked

very flustered. 'Isn't that right?'

'No, that's wrong! It's 4–9–9!' I called. 'Press 4–9–9!'

'Oh!' said Mummy Fairy. 'Now I remember.' She pressed the code – **bleep-bleep-bloop** – and said, '*Fixeridoo!* Please? *Please?*'

This time it worked. Everyone slowed back down to their normal speed. The gooey eggs flew through the air, back into their shells. The chocolate mousse slurped back into its pot. The baked beans marched back into their tin, one by one.

'Well done, Mummy Fairy,' I said. 'You did it!'

'No, Ella,' said Mummy Fairy. '*You* did it. You're going to be a brilliant fairy when you grow up.'

And she looked so pleased with me that I felt a little glow of happiness.

The people weren't fixed yet. Some were shouting and some were crying. One lady was lying on the floor yelling, 'Help! Help! The eggs are alive!'

'Time for some Fairy Dust,' said Mummy Fairy.

Mummy Fairy keeps her Fairy Dust in a secret pocket inside her handbag. She took out a handful and sprinkled it, all silvery-shiny, over everyone.

Fairy Dust is very clever. It makes you forget all the magic you've seen and everything that has happened. For ten seconds all the people in the supermarket were very still. They had sort of gone to sleep. Then . . .

'Go!' said Mummy Fairy, and they all woke up.

The supermarket was calm again.

Everyone was smiling. And our trolley was at the front of the queue.

Mummy Fairy quickly stepped behind a pile of tins. I knew she was going to become visible again.

'Where's your mummy?' said the lady at the till. 'You're not alone, are you, little girl?'

'Oh,' I said. 'Of course not. My mummy is . . . um . . . well . . . she's . . .'

'Here!' said Mummy, appearing beside me. She wasn't a fairy any more. Her shimmery wings had gone. She was just

Mummy and she winked at me. 'Oh dear, what *is* Ollie doing?'

Ollie had his thumb in his nose. He pulled out a baked bean and smiled and said, **'Weezi-weezi-weezi!'** And then he ate it.

★

On the way out we passed a cafe. The sign said, SPECIAL CHERRY MUFFINS — TODAY ONLY.

I love cherry muffins. So I said, 'Mummy, can we stop and have a cherry muffin?'

Mummy opened her mouth and I knew

she was going to say, 'Sorry, Ella, no time. Come on!'

But then she closed her mouth. She thought for a moment. And then she said, 'Yes, my love. Let's sit down and have a cherry muffin. You deserve a reward for helping me out.'

When we had got our cherry muffins, we sat at the table in the cafe.

Lenka and her mummy walked in too, and Lenka said, 'Look, Ella! I'm a butterfly!'

'You look amazing!' I said. Then I

added, 'Did you see anything strange in the supermarket?'

'Strange?' said Lenka. 'No, there was nothing strange.' And she went to sit down with her mummy.

I wanted to tell Lenka how I had remembered the code and saved the day. But I couldn't. Being a Fairy-in-Waiting is hard sometimes.

Mummy squeezed my hand and I knew she understood.

'Well done, Ella,' she said, and gave me a little secret smile.

Mummy had a cup of coffee and I had hot chocolate and Ollie had apple juice. I could see some silvery Fairy Dust in his hair. Mummy gave me my drawing book and pens and I started drawing a picture of all the flying food.

As I drew, I was thinking about being a fairy. I said, 'Mummy, do I *have* to be a fairy when I grow up?'

Mummy looked surprised. She said, 'No, Ella, of course you don't *have* to be one. But would you *like* to be one?'

I thought about the cow pooing in the

kitchen. I thought about the chocolate rain, and the woman with broccoli in her ear, and all the people screaming. I didn't want to make pooing cows and flying broccoli.

But then I thought about remembering the right magic code. And it made me feel really pleased with myself.

'Yes,' I said. 'I *do* want to be a fairy. I will be the most awesome, super-cool fairy in the world.' And I smiled at Mummy and ate my cherry muffin.

CUPCAKERIDOO!
Super-speedy magic for tea

It was Saturday and we had invited Tom and Lenka to tea. I have known Tom since I was a little baby because we were born in hospital together. Lenka only came to my school last year. Her mummy is very pretty and can make special Polish pancakes which are yummy.

Tom and Lenka are both my best friends because they like playing hide-and-seek and telling jokes. My Not-Best Friend Zoe from next door was coming over too, with her mum. My mummy and Zoe's mum think Zoe and me should be best friends because we live next door to each other, but Zoe is my Not-Best Friend because she does mean things to me. At school that week, she dropped her drink of water all over my lunch and pretended it wasn't on purpose. I wasn't looking forward to seeing her. But I *was*

looking forward to the cupcakes.

Mummy was having a FairyTube
lesson with her Fairy Tutor Fenella. She
was learning the cupcake spell.

'It's very simple,' Fenella said, on the

Fairy Computer screen. Fenella has long straight hair and oblong glasses and she says everything is very simple. She waved her wand and said, **'Cupcakeridoo!'** At once ten chocolate cupcakes appeared on the screen.

'Cupcakeridoo!' said Mummy Fairy, but, instead of cakes, ten cups appeared.

'Oh dear,' said Mummy Fairy. 'I don't know how *that* happened.'

I didn't want Mummy Fairy to make the cupcakes by magic.

'Mummy Fairy,' I said, 'I know magic is

quick. But if you magic the cupcakes,
I won't be able to lick the spoon.'

Mummy Fairy looked at her
Computawand. She looked at me. 'Good
point, Ella,' she said. 'Let's do it ourselves.'

We mixed flour, eggs, sugar, butter and
cocoa powder. I dipped my finger in the
bowl and it was *so* yummy.

'Can I eat the whole bowl of cake
mix?' I asked. 'Please, please? Just this once
as a special treat?'

'No!' said Mummy. 'You can lick the
spoon later.'

She got out the icing sugar and sprinkles. Then we heard a sound from outside. It was people clapping.

'Let's go and see what's happening,' said Mummy. She picked up my baby brother Ollie and we went outside.

Zoe and her mum were standing outside their house. A lady in a pink jacket was giving Zoe's mum a big silver award, and a man was taking a photo of them. Lots of people were watching.

'Well done!' said the lady to Zoe's mum. 'You have won Perfect House of the Year.

Your house is the tidiest and smartest house in the whole of Cherrywood! Now, everyone, come inside and see this lovely house!'

55

We followed the people inside Zoe's house. Zoe's house is always tidy, but today it was *super tidy*. All the floors were shiny. All the windows were gleaming. There was no mess anywhere. No toys, no books, no coats, *nothing*.

Our house doesn't look like that. Our house has lots of useful things, all just where you need them. Like Ollie's toys all over the floor and the pile of coats on the bench in the hall. There are books everywhere, because you never know when you might want a book.

Or a newspaper. Or an old *Fairy Times* magazine.

'Goodness,' gulped Mummy, looking around the super-tidy house. 'It's very neat. Maybe we should tidy up our house before the tea party.'

We went to say 'well done' to Zoe's mum. She looked very pleased with her silver award.

'We won the prize!' Zoe told us. 'Our house came first!'

'Well done,' said Mummy. 'And we're looking forward to the tea party later.

57

We're making chocolate cupcakes.'

'Delicious!' said Zoe's mum. 'We love chocolate cupcakes, don't we, Zoe?'

'I bet they won't be any good,' said Zoe. She said it very quietly, just to me, so that her mum wouldn't hear. 'I bet you don't even know how to make cupcakes.'

I tried to walk away. Mummy says that when people are mean you shouldn't listen.

But Zoe followed me. 'I bet your mummy will burn all the cupcakes,' she said. 'I bet you have to throw them in the bin.'

I felt furious, but I didn't show it.

'We won't burn them,' I said, and I walked very quickly back to Mummy. 'Let's go home,' I said. 'Let's finish the cupcakes.'

When we got back, we stopped in the hall. I looked at Mummy, and Mummy looked at me. Our hall wasn't as tidy as Zoe's hall. It wasn't gleaming or shiny or neat. But it was cosy.

'I *like* our house,' I said.

'So do I,' said Mummy, and she

laughed. Even so, I could tell that she was worried. I didn't want Zoe to come and laugh at our messy house.

'Let's tidy it up a *bit*,' I said.

Mummy put Ollie down and we tidied all the shoes away and hung up Ollie's hat. On the floor I found one apple core, one newspaper, one old paper bag and one jelly baby. We threw them all away. (I wanted to eat the jelly baby, but Mummy wouldn't let me.)

'There!' she said. 'Much better. Now, let's finish the cupcakes.'

But as we went into the kitchen we both gasped.

'Oh no!' said Mummy. 'What's happened?'

Ollie had happened.

Ollie had gone into the kitchen. He had climbed up on a chair and pulled down the bowl of cake mix to play with. There was cake mix in his hair, on the floor, all over the cupboards and up his nose. He had pulled down the icing sugar and sprinkles too. And he had jumbled up the newspapers on the table. The whole kitchen was a big fat mess.

'Ollie!' I shouted. 'Naughty boy!'

'Weezi-weezi-weezi!'

said Ollie, and splatted

some cake mix

on his head.

Weezi!

'Mummy!' I said. 'What are we going to do? We'll never clear this up.'

Mummy smiled. 'Of course we will!'

She stamped her feet three times, clapped her hands, wiggled her bottom and said, 'Marshmallow' . . . and **POOF!** she was Mummy Fairy.

'Which spell is best?' She wrinkled her brow. 'Let me think.'

'Once I was looking on the Spell App on your Computawand,' I told her, 'and I saw a spell called Cleaneridoo.'

'Cleaneridoo!' exclaimed Mummy Fairy. 'Of course! You are such a good Fairy-in-Waiting.'

I felt very proud of myself because I had thought of the right spell!

Mummy pressed a code on her Computawand – *bleep-bleep-bloop* – and said, **'Cleaneridoo!'** She waved her Computawand. '*Cleaneridoo!*'

For a moment nothing happened.
Then, in the corner, the mop came alive.
It whooshed over to Mummy and stood
there waiting.

A moment later, the dustpan and brush
came waddling over too. A bucket clanked
along as well, and all the washing-up
cloths jumped out of the sink and skipped
over.

My mouth fell open.

'You've made the cleaning things *magic*!'
I said.

'Yes,' said Mummy Fairy, looking pleased. 'I've made them magic and super speedy. Now, sweep the floor,' she told the mop. 'Nice and quick. Off you go.'

But the mop didn't move.

'No,' it said in a moppy sort of voice. 'I won't.'

'*What?*' Mummy Fairy stared at the mop. '*What* did you say?'

'It talked!' I gasped.

'Yes,' said Mummy Fairy.
'And it wasn't supposed to. Mop,
please stop talking and get to
work.'

'I won't,' said the mop.
'I want to play.'

'Us too!' said the cloths in
squeaky voices. 'We don't want
to clean. Cleaning is boring.
Play! Play! Play!'

'You clean the kitchen *right now*!' said Mummy Fairy, sounding cross. When Mummy goes to work, she is the boss of a big office and she is used to people doing what she says.

WON'T!

'Won't!' said the mop, and it started jigging on the spot.

'I want to play too,' said the dustpan in a dusty kind of voice. 'Let's play hide-and-seek! One . . . two . . . three . . .'

All the cleaning things started running off and hiding. The brush hid behind the bread bin. The mop hid behind Mummy Fairy.

'Stop it at once!' said Mummy Fairy, but they didn't listen. So she turned to the table. 'All right,' she said. 'Newspapers. *You* show the others how to behave. Tidy up!

Tideridoo! Tidy up!'

But the newspapers didn't
tidy themselves up. They screwed
themselves into balls and started flying
around like snowballs.

'Mummy Fairy, the spell has
gone wrong!' I cried. 'You've made
everything *naughty*!'

Mummy Fairy looked very red in the face. 'Oh dear,' she said. 'I don't know how *that* happened. Let me try again.' She pointed at the flour. 'Flour! **Tideridoo!** Put yourself away in the cupboard.'

The flour rose up in the air and started flying slowly to the cupboard.

'There, you see?' Mummy Fairy sighed with relief. 'At least one thing is behaving nicely.'

But then the flour tipped up
and started pouring all over
Mummy Fairy, Ollie and me!
'No!' shouted
Mummy Fairy.
'Naughty
flour!'

'Found you!' said the dustpan to the mop. 'Now let's play "Make a Mess"!'

The brush started brushing all the food packets out of the cupboards. 'No more cleaning! We love mess!'

'Bad brush!' said Mummy Fairy.

'*Play, play, play!*' sang the cloths, dancing around. '*Mess, mess, mess!*'

'Stop it!' cried Mummy Fairy.

'*We love mess!*' sang the cloths. '*We love mess!*'

I looked out of the window and saw Zoe coming towards the house.

'Mummy Fairy!' I shouted in a panic. 'Zoe's coming! She'll see you! She'll see the mess! She'll see *everything*!'

I ran outside to stop Zoe coming in. My heart was beating fast.

'Hello, Zoe,' I said, and I stood right in her way.

'I've got a message for your mummy,' said Zoe. 'We can't come to tea until a bit later because people are still taking photos of our house. We won Perfect House of the Year, you know.'

'I *know*,' I said.

'So where is your mummy?' Zoe tried to go past me, but I got in her way again.

'I don't know,' I said. 'Why don't you go home? Or . . . let's play in the garden.'

'I need to give your mummy the message,' said Zoe.

She tried to come past again and I grabbed her arm.

'Let go!' shouted Zoe, and she ran round me, into the house.

I ran after her and we both stopped dead at the kitchen door.

Mummy Fairy wasn't there, nor was Ollie. All the magic had stopped. The flour had stopped tipping and the cleaning things had stopped dancing. The kitchen was quiet.

But it was very, very, *very* messy.

When Zoe saw the messy kitchen, her eyes went wide. She looked at the cake mix and the flour and the newspaper balls splattered everywhere. Then she looked at me and laughed her horrible laugh.

'This is the messiest house in the *world*,' she said. 'I'm going to tell my mummy.'

She ran away, back home. I felt hot and prickly. We *didn't* have the messiest house in the world. It was only a spell gone wrong.

A moment later, Mummy came in. She wasn't a fairy any more – she was just Mummy, with cake mix smeared across her cheek and flour all over her hair. I wanted to laugh because she looked so funny. But I was a bit worried too.

'Mummy Fairy,' I said in a wobbly voice, 'did I choose the wrong spell?'

Mummy Fairy gave me a big, tight

hug. There was flour all over both of us, but I didn't care.

'You chose the perfect spell, Fairy-in-Waiting,' she said. 'I just need more practice. But for now I'm going to give my wand a rest. Let's clean up this mess ourselves.'

★

So we cleaned up. It was hard work, but we put on some music and chased each other around the kitchen with the brooms. Then we polished everything and pretended we were pirates cleaning our ship.

79

'Yo-ho-ho!' said Mummy in a pirate voice. 'Let's get this ship all shiny, sailor!'

'Aye-aye, Cap'n!' I called back.

Even Ollie rubbed the floor with a cloth.

At last the kitchen was clean and it was nearly time for Zoe and her mum and my friends to come for tea.

'You see?' said Mummy. 'We don't *always* need magic, do we? We can use our hands and brains too. That was fun, wasn't it?'

'Yes,' I said, because it was. 'But what about the cupcakes?'

'We don't need cupcakes. We've got lots of biscuits.' Mummy opened a packet and put the biscuits on a plate. 'Now go and brush your hair.'

I brushed my hair and put on a sparkly fairy clip and imagined it was my fairy crown. I thought about being a fairy one day and all the spells I would do.

But I kept thinking about the biscuits too. When I went into the kitchen, I knew I looked sad.

'Ella!' said Mummy. 'What's wrong?'

'We haven't got any cupcakes,' I said.

'We don't need cupcakes to have a tea party!'

'But Zoe said we would burn our cupcakes,' I told Mummy. 'She said we'd have to throw them in the bin. And now she'll think it's true.'

'She said that, did she?' said Mummy, and she looked cross. But then she smiled. 'All right, Ella, my darling. I promised you cupcakes so we'll have cupcakes.'

'But it's too late!' I said. Through the window I could see Zoe and her mum coming up the path.

Zoe was dragging her mum along. She was saying, 'Just wait till you see their messy house. There's stuff all over the floor! *And* they haven't got any cupcakes!'

Very quickly Mummy stamped her feet three times, clapped her hands, wiggled her bottom and said, 'Marshmallow' . . . and **POOF!** she was a fairy.

Mummy Fairy looked sternly at her Computawand. 'No nonsense now.'

Suddenly the doorbell rang.

'Oh no, Mummy Fairy!' I said. 'They're here already!'

'Hold on!' she called. 'Just coming!' Then she pressed a code on her wand – *bleep–bleep–bloop* – and said, '*Cupcakeridoo!*'

At once the kitchen was full of cupcakes. Hundreds of cupcakes. There were pink cupcakes and chocolate cupcakes and sparkly cupcakes, all on plates. There were even cupcakes that had *Tom* and *Lenka* and *Zoe* and *Ella* on them.

They were beautiful. And they smelled
like the yummiest cupcakes in the world.

I was so amazed I couldn't speak.

'Toffee apple!' said Mummy Fairy, and
instantly she was back to normal again.
She went into the hall, opened the front
door and smiled at Zoe and her mum.

'Come in!' she said. 'Welcome to our
tea party.'

When Zoe came into the kitchen and
saw all the cupcakes, her mouth dropped
open.

'The house is looking beautiful!' said

Zoe's mum. 'So neat and tidy. And look at all these wonderful cupcakes! *You* could win the Perfect House of the Year Award!'

'I don't think our house is perfect,' said Mummy with a smile. 'But we still love it. Don't we, Ella?'

Zoe looked at me with tiny, angry eyes and gave me a push when she knew her mum wasn't looking.

'I *know* the kitchen was messy,' she said. 'I *know* the cupcake mix was on the floor. How did you make all those cupcakes so quickly?'

But I didn't reply. I thought about Mummy Fairy and the talking mop. I thought about the naughty flour and the dancing cloths and the newspapers flying like snowballs. I thought about polishing the kitchen and pretending to be a pirate. I thought about my best friends Tom and Lenka, who would be arriving any minute. And I smiled my nicest smile.

'Here you are, Zoe,' I said. 'Have a cupcake.'

GET BETTERIDOO!
How not to cure Fairy Flu with a bouncing bed

One morning I went into Mummy's bedroom and stopped in shock. She had red spots all over her face and was blowing her nose.

'Mummy,' I gasped, 'I think you're ill!'

'I know,' said Mummy in a croaky voice. 'I need some medicine.'

She tried all the different medicines in the cupboard, but nothing worked. At last Daddy called the doctor.

The doctor came and looked at Mummy's spots. He took her temperature and peered into her ears.

'You have a very unusual kind of flu,' he said. 'You must rest and then you will get better.'

'Rest?' said Mummy.

'Yes,' said the doctor. 'Rest.'

Mummy doesn't like rest. She likes working hard and having fun and being busy. As soon as the doctor had gone she got out of bed. Looking very wobbly, she stamped her feet three times, clapped her hands, wiggled her bottom and said, 'Marshmallow' . . . and **POOF!** she was Mummy Fairy. But her wings were all dull and droopy, and her crown didn't shimmer.

'I am going to cure myself with magic,' she told Daddy and me.

'I think that's a bad idea,' said Daddy,

looking alarmed. But Mummy Fairy pointed the Computawand at herself and pressed a code – **bleep–bleep–bloop**. 'Get Betteridoo!'

We all waited. But Mummy Fairy's spots didn't go away and her nose was still runny. Her wings drooped even further.

'Do you feel any better?' asked Daddy.

'No,' said Mummy. 'I don't know *what's* wrong. I'm going to look at the Fairy Doctor App.'

She started scrolling down her screen,

searching for a spell. Just then, Granny came in.

'Oh dear, you have Fairy Flu,' she said as soon as she saw Mummy Fairy. 'I'm afraid there is no spell for Fairy Flu. If you try to cure it with magic, you'll make it worse. You must drink lemon squash and rest. And you must definitely *not* try any more magic.'

'You probably need a good rest,' said Daddy.

'I don't *want* a good rest,' said Mummy Fairy. 'I want to get better.' She looked very, very cross. 'Toffee apple,' she said, and went back to bed.

★

After lunch I went to see how Mummy was feeling. She was sitting up in bed all alone in her nightie, drinking lemon squash and reading her Spell Book.

Mummy hardly ever gets out her Spell Book. It is very old and the writing is very tiny and the pages are very thin. It was written hundreds of years ago by the Old, Old Fairies. Nowadays most fairies have Computawands to tell them their spells instead. But, even so, every fairy has a Spell Book. I can't wait until I'm old enough to have one.

'Why are you reading your Spell Book?' I asked. 'Granny said you mustn't do any magic.'

But Mummy took no notice. 'Here we are,' she said. 'I knew I'd find something! A spell to make you feel cooler. That's exactly what I need.' She got out of bed, stamped her feet three times, clapped her hands, wiggled her bottom and said, 'Marshmallow' . . . and **POOF!** she was a fairy.

Then she pointed her Computawand at herself, pressed a code – **bleep-bleep-bloop** – and said, 'Cooleridoo!'

At once snow started falling on her head.

'Oops,' said Mummy Fairy. 'I don't know how *that* happened. **Stoperidoo!'**

She pointed the Computawand at herself, but the snow didn't stop.

'Mummy Fairy!' I said. 'You'll freeze! And your head will turn into a snowball! Shall I call Aunty Jo? Maybe she can cure you.'

'No!' said Mummy Fairy, looking a bit cross. 'I don't need Aunty Jo. I can do this *myself.'*

Mummy Fairy put on a woolly hat and flipped through the book. 'Let me try something else,' she said. 'Here we are – a spell for strength. **Strongeridoo!**'

At once Mummy Fairy's arms changed. They got big and muscly like a champion weightlifter's.

'Oops,' said Mummy Fairy. 'I don't know how *that* happened. I wonder how strong I am.'

She reached over and took hold of me with one hand, then lifted me up over her head.

'Help!' I cried.

'I'm really super strong,' said Mummy.

'Isn't that cool?'

I felt very strange, balanced on Mummy's hand, looking down at her head.

'Mummy Fairy,' I gasped, 'I think you should stop doing magic.'

'But I'm sure I can cure myself,' she said, putting me down again. 'I just need to find the right spell. Look, here's a cure for spots. *Spotseridoo!*' She pressed a code on her Computawand – **bleep–bleep–bloop** – and all her spots disappeared.

'There!' said Mummy Fairy. 'You see?

It worked. I knew it would.'

A moment later, the spots came back, but now they were bright green. They got bigger and bigger, till her whole face was green.

'Oh dear,' said Mummy Fairy. 'It didn't work after all.'

Now Mummy Fairy had muscly arms, a green face and snow falling on her head. I didn't think she looked at all better. I sat down on the bed and said, 'Mummy Fairy, why don't you just rest like Granny said?'

But Mummy Fairy wasn't listening. 'Here we are.' She turned to another page in the Spell Book. 'A spell for feeling bouncy. *That* will make me stop feeling ill.' Mummy Fairy pointed the Computawand at herself, pressed a code – **bleep-bleep-bloop** – and said, 'Bounceridoo!'

At once the bed gave a little bounce. I looked at Mummy Fairy, and Mummy

103

Fairy looked at me. The bed bounced again.

'Oops,' said Mummy Fairy. 'That's not what I meant by "bouncy".'

The bed gave a bigger bounce and I clung on to Mummy. Then it gave lots of bounces – *bouncy bouncy bouncy*. It was going higher and higher, up to the ceiling and down again. I felt as if we were on a trampoline.

'Mummy Fairy!'

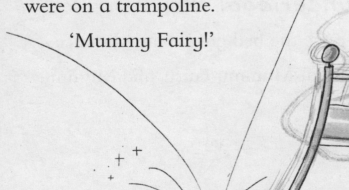

I cried.
'I think I'm
going to fall off!'
'Hold on tight,
Ella!' said Mummy
Fairy. 'I'll try to stop it.
Stoperidoo! Stop,
you silly bed!'

But the bed was still bouncing. All of a sudden it gave a huge bounce and flew towards the window. The window was getting bigger and bigger.

'What's happening?' I said.

'It must be part of the spell,' said Mummy Fairy. 'Oh dear. Hold on . . .'

We sailed through the window, then down to the ground . . . and *bounce*. We were outside, flying up into the air. Then down again and *bounce*.

The duvet was flapping. I could feel wind in my hair. I shouted, 'Wheeee!' as we shot up again. Then I started laughing because bouncing was *fun*.

'What are we going to do?' said Mummy Fairy. 'We can't just keep bouncing all day!'

The bed landed on someone's lawn and then . . . **bounce**. Up we shot, into the air. **'Stoperidoo!'** shouted Mummy Fairy, but the bed didn't stop bouncing.

We bounced ten more times. Then the bed seemed to get tired. It made stretchy shapes and yawny sounds. It landed on top of a house and stopped.

Mummy Fairy and I looked at each other. We were stuck on the roof of a house. Mummy Fairy was in her nightie. How were we going to get home?

'My head is really cold,' said Mummy Fairy. 'I must get rid of this snow.' She pointed the Computawand at herself and cried, **'Heateridoo!'**

But the snow didn't stop falling on her head. Nothing had happened.

'Oh dear,' said Mummy Fairy. 'I really wanted some warmth.'

Suddenly I heard a **roar** and I screamed.

108

A little red dragon was flying towards us. It had a pointed nose and sharp claws. It sat on Mummy Fairy's shoulder and breathed out fire with a roary sound.

'Mummy Fairy!' I said. 'There's a dragon on your shoulder!'

'Not *that* kind of warmth!' said Mummy Fairy. 'Shoo!' she said to the dragon, but it wouldn't go.

'Can we keep him as a pet?' I begged. 'Can we call it Roary? I think Daddy would love him. You know I have always wanted a pet.'

'Daddy would *not* love him!' said Mummy Fairy. 'We need to get rid of this dragon and go home!'

Then I saw a man. He was on the roof of the next-door house, fixing the tiles.

'Look, Mummy Fairy!' I said. 'There's a man. He can help us.'

'I'll talk to him,' said Mummy Fairy.
'Excuse me!' she called, waving her arms.
'Coo-eee!'

The man turned round. When he saw
Mummy Fairy, he nearly fell off the roof
in shock.

'Help!' he shouted. 'It's a monster!
It's a monster with a green face and
muscly arms and a dragon on its
shoulder!'

'I'm not a monster!' said Mummy
Fairy, and the dragon roared.

The man looked even more scared.

'It can talk!' he said. 'Help! Save me from the monster!'

'I'm not a monster!' Mummy Fairy was cross.

'Please don't eat me,' begged the man.

'I'm not going to eat you!' said Mummy Fairy. 'Why would I eat you?'

'Because you're a monster!' said the man.

He looked so scared of Mummy Fairy that I couldn't help giggling.

Just then I heard a voice behind me. 'And *what* exactly are you doing?'

It was Granny Fairy. She was flying
through the air with her shimmery
wings and gold crown with blue stones,
frowning. She sat down on
the bed, fluttering her
wings.

'It's a giant butterfly!' said the man on
the other roof. 'Help! It's a giant man-
eating butterfly!'

'Stilleridoo!' said Granny Fairy, and the man went very still and quiet.

Then Granny Fairy looked hard at Mummy Fairy.

'Mummy Fairy,' she said, 'Daddy phoned me and said that you and Ella were missing. He was very worried and now I am worried too. What are you doing out here? Why have you got a green face, muscly arms, falling snow and a dragon on your shoulder?'

Mummy Fairy looked ashamed.

'I thought I might find a magic cure for Fairy Flu,' she said.

'There *isn't* a magic cure for Fairy Flu,' said Granny Fairy. 'I've already told you that. You just have to wait and be patient.'

'I don't like waiting and being patient,' said Mummy Fairy.

'I know,' said Granny Fairy. 'Nobody does. But that's life. Now, I will clear up all your silly magic mistakes for you. And I'm going to use Fairy Dust on all the people who saw your bouncing bed, so they will think it was a dream. Including this poor

117

man.' She pointed to the man on the roof.

'Thank you,' said Mummy Fairy.

'And in return you must promise me you will drink lemon squash and *rest*,' said Granny Fairy. 'Then you will get better.'

'I promise,' said Mummy Fairy. 'Thank you.' Then she looked at her muscly weightlifter's arms. 'Do you think I should keep these?' she said. 'They're so strong.'

'No,' said Granny Fairy. 'You wouldn't fit into any of your clothes.' She waved her wand and said, **'Fixeridoo!'**

A moment later, everything was right again. We were back in our house, on the bed. Mummy just had ordinary red spots like before and normal arms and no snow falling on her. And she was asleep.

I looked around, but Roary the dragon was gone too.

'Bye-bye, Roary,' I said sadly. Then I put the Spell Book away and crept out of the room.

A week later, Mummy was better. Her spots were all gone. She got out of bed and had breakfast and put on her office suit to go to work.

When we went outside, Zoe's mum was in the garden with Zoe. They were planting some bulbs.

'I am growing some daffodils,' Zoe's mum told us. 'They will be very pretty. But it will take a long time.

We must be patient.' Then she sighed.
'I don't like being patient.'

'Nor do I,' said Mummy.

'Waiting is so boring,' said Zoe's mum.

'Yes,' said Mummy. 'It is. But sometimes waiting is better than rushing. Isn't it, Ella?'

I thought about Mummy rushing to get better. I thought about her green spots, the snow, the bouncing bed and the man who thought she was a monster.

Then I smiled at her and said, 'Yes, Mummy. Sometimes waiting is better than rushing.'

REWINDERIDOO!
The best sports day ever — again and again . . .

One day Mummy came to my room and gave me a pair of trainers.

'What are those for?' I asked.

'It's sports day later,' she said. 'These are for you to practise your jumping!'

I put them on, then ran out to the grass

in the front garden and went step, step, **jump**. But my shoelaces were too long and I tripped over them. I landed with a **thud** on the grass and bumped my nose. I'm not very good at sports, but Miss Amy says I am a trier.

At that moment my Not-Best Friend Zoe ran past in her new trainers. Zoe lives next door to

me and she always says mean things. Today she just pointed at me and laughed her horrible laugh and ran into her house.

I didn't say anything because Mummy says you should ignore unkind people, but I felt hot and a bit sad. I brushed the mud off my knees and tried to tie my laces properly, but they got into a big tangle. I *hate* shoelaces.

'Ready for sports day?' said Zoe's mum. She was going into her house with some shopping. 'Oh dear, what a pickle your laces are in!'

Zoe's mum went inside. Then Mummy came out and saw me trying to do up my laces.

'Come on, darling!' she said. 'It's time to go. Let's speed you up.'

She looked around to make sure no one could see. Then she stamped her feet three times, clapped her hands, wiggled her bottom and said, 'Marshmallow' . . . and **POOF!** she was a fairy.

She pointed at my shoes with her Computawand and said, *'Laceridoo!'*

At once my laces
started moving on their own.
But they didn't knot themselves
neatly. They flew into the air
and went to hang on the apple tree.
The next minute all Daddy's shoelaces
came flying out of the window and
went to hang on the tree too.
They looked like
spaghetti
and I started
giggling.

'Oops,' said Mummy Fairy, and prodded her Computawand. 'I don't know how *that* happened.'

Just then, Aunty Jo came out of the front door. She was going to come and watch me at sports day too. Aunty Jo is very good at magic and her house is full of silver prizes from the Fairy Awards. She saw the laces waving in the tree and shook her head.

'Tragic,' she said. 'Let me fix that for you.' She stamped her feet three times, clapped her hands, wiggled her bottom

and said, 'Sherbet lemon' . . . and
POOF! she was a fairy, just
like Mummy, with silver wings and
a crown. Aunty Jo Fairy pointed
her Computawand at the tree
and said, *'Fixeridoo!'*
At once my laces zoomed
back into my shoes and
tied themselves into
a neat knot. All
Daddy's laces sailed
back in through the
window.

'Thank you, Aunty Jo Fairy,' I said.

'Well done, Jo,' said Mummy Fairy, although she didn't look very pleased.

'My pleasure,' said Aunty Jo Fairy. 'And now, Ella, what about a little Twinkletoes spell to make you run nice and fast?'

I liked the idea of a Twinkletoes spell.

'Yes please!' I said.

But Mummy Fairy stepped forward before Aunty Jo Fairy could point her wand. 'No!' she said. 'That's cheating! We do not cheat in this family. Do we, Ella?'

I knew Mummy Fairy was right. Cheating was wrong. But I really, really wanted a Twinkletoes spell to help me. Maybe then I could even win a race.

'It's just one tiny spell,' said Aunty Jo Fairy to Mummy Fairy. 'Don't you want Ella to win all the races?'

'Not by cheating,' said Mummy Fairy firmly.

'Look!' I said. 'Zoe's coming back. She'll see you!'

At once Mummy Fairy and Aunty Jo Fairy stepped behind a bush to hide.

131

When Zoe reached our garden, she stopped. She peered at the bush and narrowed her eyes.

'What was that?' she said. 'Is someone hiding?'

'No!' I said. 'It's nothing. Maybe a squirrel.'

'Oh.' Zoe looked at the bush again, then turned away. 'Well, I'll see you at sports

day, Ella. Oh no, I *won't* see you. Because
I'll be at the front of every race and you'll
be at the back. You're going to lose every
single one.' She stuck out her tongue and
ran off.

I was too cross to reply.

As Aunty Jo Fairy came out from
behind the bush, she looked furious.

'What a horrid girl!' she said. 'Ella, if
only I could give you the Twinkletoes
spell. You would twinkle and whizz along
like a rocket!'

'Mummy Fairy, *please* can I twinkle

133

and whizz?' I said. 'Just in one race?'

'No,' said Mummy Fairy, looking crossly at Aunty Jo Fairy. 'You must promise me, you will not put any spells on Ella to help her win.'

'All right,' said Aunty Jo Fairy, crossing her arms.

'Not even a tiny one,' said Mummy Fairy.

'I promise!' said Aunty Jo Fairy. 'Not even a tiny one.'

But when Mummy Fairy wasn't looking, Aunty Jo Fairy winked at me.

134

★

The sports day was in the big field behind my school.

'Welcome to sports day!' said Miss Amy. 'Now, let's begin!'

All the parents were standing at the side, watching the races. The first race was running, and my whole class was lined up. I reached down to touch my feet, but they didn't feel twinkly or whizzy – they just felt normal. Aunty Jo hadn't put a spell on me after all. She must have listened to Mummy. I felt a bit disappointed.

'On your marks, get set . . . *go*!' shouted
Miss Amy, and we all began to run. I was
running as fast as I could and I looked
round to see where the others were.

I couldn't believe my eyes. They were

all running slowly. Really, really slowly.
Even Zoe.

'Come on, Zoe!' her mum was shouting.
'Faster!'

'I'm trying!' yelled Zoe. 'My legs won't
move!'

Zoe and all the other children in the race looked like slow-motion people on TV. They looked so silly that I started to laugh.

'Ella!' shouted Aunty Jo. 'Run!'

I ran to the end of the race, all on my own. I was the winner! Everyone else was miles and miles behind me.

'Well done, Ella!' said my friend Tom as he ran up to the finishing line. He was panting and red in the face. 'My legs felt so weird. I tried and tried, but I couldn't run fast.'

138

'Clever girl!' said Aunty Jo, and she gave me a huge hug. 'You'll get a gold medal!'

Zoe was furious. 'How did *you* win?' she said. 'It's not fair. *I'm* the best at running.'

'Very good, Ella!' said Mummy Fairy, but she gave Aunty Jo a hard stare. 'What happened to the others, I wonder?'

'I have *no* idea,' said Aunty Jo. 'Now, it's time for the long jump.'

We all lined up in front of the long jump. It was a tray of sand and the person who jumped the furthest would be the winner. When we did the practice

139

yesterday, I crashed so hard on my bottom that everyone laughed. I hoped I wouldn't crash like that today.

My friend Lenka was going first and she got ready. She ran to the sand tray, **step**, **step** . . . but then she jumped backwards. She jumped the *wrong way*.

'Oh dear!' said Miss Amy, looking surprised. 'Lenka, you should have jumped forward. I'm afraid you don't get any score. Tom, it's your turn.'

Tom ran towards the sand tray. **Step**, **step** . . . and then he jumped backwards too!

Everyone started laughing.

'I don't understand!' said Tom. 'I wanted to jump forward, but my legs just jumped backwards!'

All the children kept jumping backwards. All the teachers were calling, 'This way! Jump *forward*!'

Then it was my turn. I ran at the sand tray. **Step, step, leap!** I landed in the sand with a crash and Aunty Jo cheered.

'Very good!' said Miss Amy. 'As no one else has jumped the right way, you are the winner, Ella.'

'Hooray!' yelled Aunty Jo, waving her arms. 'Ella's the winner! Ella gets another gold medal!'

I didn't feel as happy as I had expected. I didn't feel like a proper winner. I had only won because everyone else went backwards.

'Wait!' shouted Mummy Fairy. I was amazed because Mummy had become a fairy in front of everyone. She waved her Computawand and said, **'Freezeridoo!'**

At once everyone except Mummy Fairy and Aunty Jo and me went still. All the teachers and parents and children were like statues – and as I looked at them, I started to giggle. Tom was standing on one leg. Mr Wilson, the head teacher, was scratching his head. Zoe had her finger up her nose.

143

No one could see or hear us.

Mummy Fairy was very cross with

Aunty Jo.

'What have you done?' she said. 'You

promised not to put a spell on Ella.'

'I *didn't* put a spell on Ella,' said Aunty Jo. 'I put spells on all the *other* children. First a Slow-down spell, then a Go-backwards spell. Aren't I clever?'

She winked at me, but I didn't know whether to smile back.

'No, you are *not* clever!' said Mummy. 'I told you not to use any spells. I *never* use magic at Ella's school.'

'That's because –' Aunty Jo stopped.

'What?' said Mummy Fairy. 'Because what?'

'Because you aren't very good at magic,' said Aunty Jo.

Mummy Fairy was breathing hard. I think she was trying not to get angry. But *I* felt angry.

'Mummy Fairy *is* good at magic!' I said to Aunty Jo. 'She can fly! And she can turn invisible! She's the best Mummy Fairy in the world!'

'Sorry.' Aunty Jo bit her lip. 'I didn't mean to say that.'

'Perhaps I am not as good at magic as you,' said Mummy Fairy to Aunty Jo.

146

'Perhaps I don't have any silver cups. But I try hard. And Ella tries hard at sports. And that is what sports day is all about. Trying hard. Isn't it, Ella?'

I nodded, even though I still really wanted a gold medal.

Aunty Jo looked down at the grass. 'I was wrong,' she said. 'I shouldn't have done any spells. And I shouldn't have been rude about your magic,' she said to Mummy Fairy. 'I'm very sorry.'

Then I had an idea. I remembered a spell I had seen on Mummy's Spell App.

'Mummy Fairy,' I said. 'Could we start the sports day again, properly? Could we use the Rewinderidoo spell?'

Mummy Fairy's eyes sparkled at me. 'That's a brilliant idea, Fairy-in-Waiting!' she said. 'We'll go back to the beginning of the sports day and start again *with no spells*. OK?'

I nodded. 'OK.'

'OK,' said Aunty Jo. 'Good luck, Ella!'

Mummy Fairy got out her Computawand and looked at it. Then she stopped.

'The Rewinderidoo spell is very tricky,' she said. I could see she was a bit nervous. 'I've never done it before without help. I hope it goes right.' Then she looked at Aunty Jo. 'I don't suppose . . .'

'Let's do it together,' said Aunty Jo, and she winked at me. She stamped her feet three times, clapped her hands, wiggled her bottom and said, 'Sherbet lemon' . . . and **POOF!** she was Aunty Jo Fairy, with shimmering wings and a diamond crown and a shiny Computawand.

Together, Mummy Fairy and Aunty

Jo Fairy pressed the special code on their screens – **bleep–bleep–bloop**.

'Rewinderidoo!' they shouted together, and everything started going backwards. It was like when they do a

rewind on TV. I could see Zoe running
backwards. I could see Lenka eating
a biscuit backwards. Then I saw Tom
blowing his nose backwards. That made
me laugh.

Suddenly the rewinding stopped. We were in the field at the beginning of sports day again. Mummy and Aunty Jo were back to normal.

'Welcome to sports day!' said Miss Amy. 'Now, let's begin!'

★

This time, no one ran slowly or jumped backwards. Zoe won three gold medals for running, long jump and high jump, and I made myself clap hard when she went up to get them. Zoe is very good at running, even if she isn't a nice person.

Then it was the three-legged race. I was with Tom. Lenka was with Zoe. Our legs were tied together and we had to run in time with each other.

'Now, children, don't rush,' said Miss Amy before the race started. 'You have to work as a team.'

When the race began, Tom and I started counting. 'One-*two*. One-*two*.' We weren't very fast, but we ran along in time with each other. I could hear Zoe yelling, 'Hurry up, stupid!' to Lenka. The next minute Zoe and Lenka had fallen over on the grass.

But Tom and I didn't look back. We didn't need to shout at each other because we were friends and friends don't shout. We just kept on going, 'One-*two*, one-*two* . . .' until suddenly we had crossed the line.

We had won the race!

Miss Amy gave Tom and me each a shiny gold medal. Aunty Jo and Mummy waved their arms and cheered and hugged each other. And I felt really happy. I had won a race *properly*.

'Well done, Ella!' Tom said to me.

'Well done, Tom!' I said to Tom, and we both laughed.

'Let's go and get some ice cream as a treat!' said Mummy. 'Tom, you come too.'

Then Zoe came up to us. She looked

at me with small, angry blue eyes. 'How did *you* win a race, Ella? You're no good at sports,' she hissed so nobody could hear but me.

I thought about Aunty Jo's magic spells. I thought about running faster than everyone else, and jumping the right way when everyone else went backwards. Then I thought about winning the race with Tom, without any magic at all. And I thought about Mummy Fairy and Aunty Jo doing the Rewinderidoo spell together.

'I won because Tom and I are friends and we worked as a team,' I said. 'That is the *best* way to win.' And I stroked my shiny gold medal and smiled.

TEST YOUR

Fairy Skills

Read on for lots of
fun activities!

DESIGN YOUR OWN FAIRY

Remember when Ella imagined herself as the most awesome, super-cool fairy in the world? Now draw what you'd look like as a fairy in Ella's thought bubble – be as creative as you can!

FINDERIDOO!

Can you spot Mummy Fairy's favourite

things in the word search?

(Answers on page 166.)

COMPUTAWAND

CUPCAKE

DADDY

ELLA

GRANNY

FAIRYTUBE

MAGIC

MARSHMALLOW

OLLIE

SPELLS

C	O	M	P	U	T	A	W	A	N	D	C
M	S	L	L	E	P	S	Y	T	W	Z	U
F	A	β	K	G	T	G	R	U	W	V	P
A	G	R	H	G	R	M	I	β	D	U	C
I	V	R	S	A	Y	E	A	E	R	I	A
R	C	T	N	H	I	D	F	L	G	E	K
Y	S	N	C	J	M	C	D	A	N	A	E
T	Y	T	T	H	O	A	M	A	V	P	U
U	L	U	E	X	Z	Z	L	H	D	V	K
β	F	L	L	I	N	O	L	L	I	E	P
E	H	U	L	W	Z	Y	T	D	O	X	β
O	C	M	A	β	D	R	J	A	P	W	E

161

SPOTERIDOO!

Can you spot the eight

differences in the pictures?

(Answers on page 166.)

FAIRY CAKE RECIPE

Bake your own cupcakes, exactly like Mummy Fairy
and Ella's! Just make sure you get a grown-up to help,
especially with a hot oven. (They don't have to be a fairy!)

INGREDIENTS
- ★ 110g/4oz soft butter or margarine
- ★ 110g/4oz caster sugar
- ★ 2 free-range eggs, lightly beaten
- ★ 1 teaspoon vanilla extract
- ★ 110g/4oz self-raising flour
- ★ 1-2 tablespoons milk

FOR BUTTERCREAM ICING:
- ★ 140g/5oz butter, softened
- ★ 280g/10oz icing sugar
- ★ 1-2 tablespoons milk
- ★ a few drops of food colouring

METHOD

 Preheat the oven to 180°C/350°F/Gas 4 and line a 12-hole muffin tin with paper cases.

 Cream the butter and sugar together in a bowl until pale. Beat in the eggs a little at a time and stir in the vanilla extract.

 Fold in the flour using a large metal spoon, adding a little milk until the mixture is of a dropping consistency. Spoon the mixture into the paper cases until they are half full.

 Bake in the oven for 10–15 minutes, or until golden-brown on top and a skewer inserted into one of the cakes comes out clean. Set aside to cool for 10 minutes, then remove from the tin and cool on a wire rack.

 For the buttercream icing, beat the butter in a large bowl until soft. Add half the icing sugar and beat until smooth.

 Then add the remaining icing sugar with one tablespoon of milk, adding more milk if necessary, until the mixture is smooth and creamy.

 Add the food colouring and mix until well combined.

 Spoon the icing on to the cupcakes and sprinkle with your own favourite magical toppings.

ANSWERS

FINDERIDOO!

C	O	M	P	U	T	A	W	A	N	D	C
M	S	L	L	E	P	S	Y	T	W	Z	U
F	A	B	K	G	T	G	R	U	W	V	P
A	G	R	H	G	R	M	I	B	D	U	C
I	V	R	S	A	Y	E	A	E	R	I	A
R	C	T	N	H	I	D	F	L	G	E	K
Y	S	N	C	J	M	C	D	A	N	A	E
T	Y	T	T	H	O	A	M	A	V	P	U
U	L	U	E	X	Z	Z	L	H	D	V	K
B	F	L	L	I	N	O	L	L	I	E	P
E	H	U	L	W	Z	Y	T	D	O	X	B
O	C	M	A	B	D	R	J	A	P	W	E

SPOTERIDOO!

166

Get ready for new
magical adventures!

Mummy Fairy and Me

Fairy-in-Waiting

Coming summer 2018

*Mummy Fairy stories are also
available in audiobook*

ABOUT SOPHIE KINSELLA

Sophie Kinsella is a bestselling author and the adventures of Ella and Mummy Fairy are her first stories for children. Her books for grown-ups have sold over thirty-eight million copies worldwide and have been translated into more than forty languages. They include the Shopaholic series and other titles such as *Can You Keep a Secret?*, *The Undomestic Goddess*, *My Not So Perfect Life*, *Surprise Me*, and *Finding Audrey* for young adults.

You can find out more about Sophie's books on her website:

www.sophiekinsella.co.uk